Books should be returned or renewed by the
last date stamped above

_____

_____

_____

Awarded for excellence
to Arts & Libraries

Kent
County
Council

First published in 2009
by Wayland

This paperback edition published in 2010 by Wayland

Wayland
338 Euston Road
London NW1 3BH

Wayland Australia
Level 17/207 Kent Street
Sydney, NSW 2000

Series Editor: Louise John
Editor: Katie Powell
Cover design: Paul Cherrill
Design: D.R.ink
Consultant: Shirley Bickler

A CIP catalogue record for this book is available from the British Library.

ISBN 9780750259118 (hbk)
ISBN 9780750259293 (pbk)

Printed in China

Wayland is a division of Hachette Children's Books,
an Hachette UK Company

www.hachette.co.uk

Is it for me?

Written by Claire Llewellyn
Illustrated by Polona Lovšin

WAYLAND

I like this card.

Is it for me?

No. It is for the baby.

I like this blanket.

Is it for me?

No. It is for the baby.

I like this hat.

Is it for me?

No. It is for the baby.

9

I like this teddy.

Is it for me?

I like this rattle.

Is it for me?

No. It is for the baby.

I like this ball.

Is it for me?

I like this duck.

Is it for me?

No. It is for the baby.

17

I like this dog.

Is it for me?

No. It is for the baby.

I like this book.

This book is for **me**.

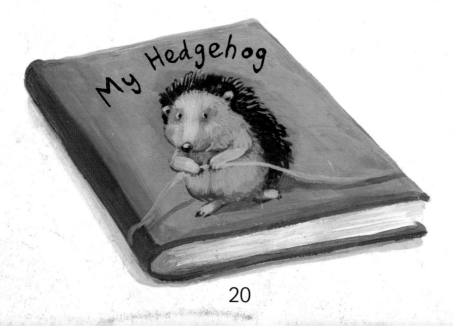

It is for me **and** the baby.

Guiding a First Read
Is it for me?

It is important to talk through the book with the child before they read it alone. This prepares them for the way the story unfolds, and allows them to enjoy the pictures as you both talk naturally, using the language they will later encounter when reading. Read them the brief overview, and then follow the suggestions below:

The high frequency words in this title are:

I   is   it   for   like   me   no   the

1. Talking through the book

The baby has lots of new things that his brother likes.

> Let's read the title: **Is it for me?**
> Turn to page 4. The boy says to his Mum,
> "I like this card. Is it for me?"
> But Mum says, "No. It is for the baby."
>
> Now turn to page 6. What do you think
> the boy says on this page?

Continue to read the book, with the child looking at the illustrations.

> At last the boy has a present on p20.
> He says, "This book is for me.
> It is for me and the baby."

2. A first reading of the book

Ask the child to read the book independently and point carefully underneath each word (tracking), while thinking about the story.

Work with the child, prompting them and praising their careful tracking, attempts to correct themselves and their knowledge of letters and sounds, for example:

Good, you said 'is' and then changed it to 'I'. You made that sound just like a question. You must have seen the question mark.

3. Follow-up activities

· Select a high frequency word, as listed on p22, and ask the child to find it throughout the book. Discuss the shape of the letters and the letter sounds.

· To memorise the word, ask the child to write it in the air, then write it repeatedly on a whiteboard or on paper, leaving a space between each attempt.

· Alternate writing the new word starting with a capital letter, and then with a lower-case letter.

4. Encourage

· Rereading of the book many times.

· Drawing a picture based on the story.

· Writing a sentence using the practised word.

START READING is a series of highly enjoyable books for beginner readers. **The books have been carefully graded to match the Book Bands widely used in schools.** This enables readers to be sure they choose books that match their own reading ability.

Look out for the Band colour on the book in our Start Reading logo.

The Bands are:

	Pink Band 1A and 1B
	Red Band 2
	Yellow Band 3
	Blue Band 4
	Green Band 5
	Orange Band 6
	Turquoise Band 7
	Purple Band 8
	Gold Band 9

START READING books can be read independently or shared with an adult. They promote the enjoyment of reading through satisfying stories supported by fun illustrations.

Claire Llewellyn has written many books for children. Some of them are about real things like animals and the Moon, others are storybooks. Claire has two children, but they are getting too big for stories like this one. She hopes you will enjoy reading her stories instead.

Polona Lovšin was born in Ljubljana, Slovenia in 1973. She graduated from the Academy of Fine Arts in Ljubljana. Polona loves to draw people, especially children and finds that each new book brings many challenges but lots of fun, too!